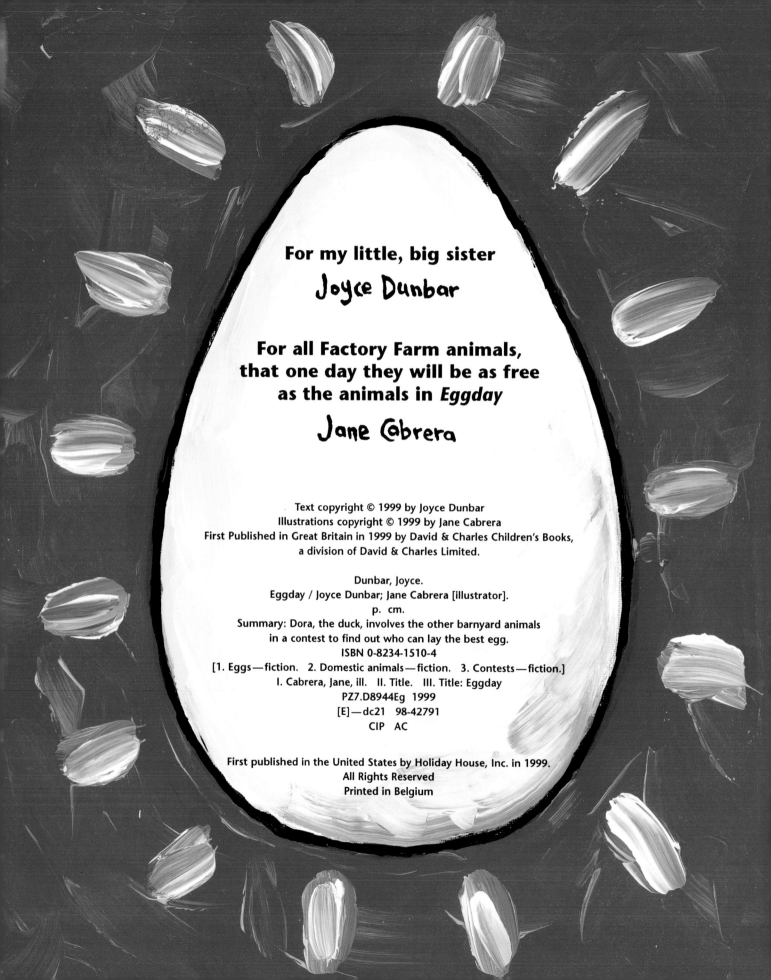

For my little, big sister
Joyce Dunbar

**For all Factory Farm animals,
that one day they will be as free
as the animals in *Eggday***
Jane Cabrera

Text copyright © 1999 by Joyce Dunbar
Illustrations copyright © 1999 by Jane Cabrera
First Published in Great Britain in 1999 by David & Charles Children's Books,
a division of David & Charles Limited.

Dunbar, Joyce.
Eggday / Joyce Dunbar; Jane Cabrera [illustrator].
p. cm.
Summary: Dora, the duck, involves the other barnyard animals
in a contest to find out who can lay the best egg.
ISBN 0-8234-1510-4
[1. Eggs—fiction.   2. Domestic animals—fiction.   3. Contests—fiction.]
I. Cabrera, Jane, ill.   II. Title.   III. Title: Eggday
PZ7.D8944Eg 1999
[E]—dc21   98-42791
CIP   AC

First published in the United States by Holiday House, Inc. in 1999.

Eggday

Joyce Dunbar ☀ Illustrated by Jane C@brera

Holiday House ☀ New York

Dora, the duck, said to Pogson, the pig, "Tomorrow is Eggday."

"What's Eggday?" asked Pogson.

"We are having a best egg competition," said Dora.

"But what can I bring?" asked Pogson.
"A pig egg," said Dora, and she
waddled over to tell Humphrey, the horse.

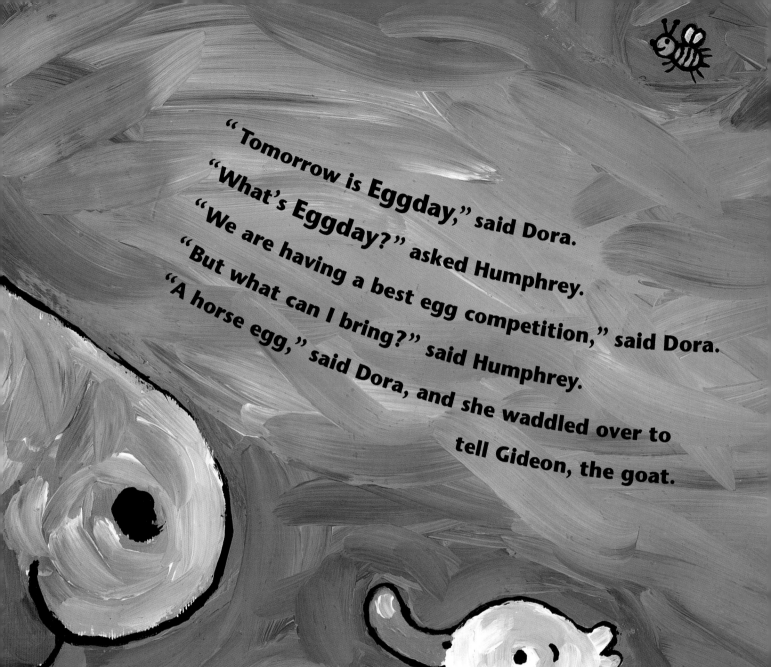

"Tomorrow is Eggday," said Dora.

"What's Eggday?" asked Humphrey.

"We are having a best egg competition," said Dora.

"But what can I bring?" said Humphrey.

"A horse egg," said Dora, and she waddled over to tell Gideon, the goat.

"Tomorrow is Eggday," said Dora.

"What's Eggday?" asked Gideon.

"We are having a best egg competition," said Dora.

"But what can I bring?" asked Gideon.

"A goat egg," said Dora, and she

waddled back to her nest.

"Where will I get a pig egg?" Pogson, the pig, asked Humphrey, the horse.

"Where will I get a horse egg?"
Humphrey, the horse, asked
Gideon, the goat.

"Where will I get a goat egg?"
Gideon, the goat, asked himself.

Hetty Hen came to see what was wrong.

"What's all the fuss?" she asked.

"It's **Eggday** tomorrow," said Pogson. "I am trying to lay a pig egg."

"But pigs don't lay eggs," said Hetty. "Pigs have piglets. And you're not even a sow."

"And I am trying to lay a horse egg," said Humphrey.

"But horses don't lay eggs," said Hetty. "Horses have foals. And you're not even a mare."

"And I am trying to lay a goat egg," said Gideon.

"But goats don't lay eggs," said Hetty. "Goats have kids. And you're a billy goat, not a nanny goat."

"But Dora says it's Eggday tomorrow," said Pogson.

"What's Eggday?" asked Hetty Hen.

"We are having a best egg competition,"
said Pogson, "and we all have to bring an egg."
"Wait here a moment," said Hetty,
"and I'll see what I can find in my coop."

Hetty came back with three eggs.

"Here's one for you," she said to Pogson.

"Give it a short curly tail and it will look like a pig egg."

"Here's one for you, Humphrey," said Hetty.

"Give it a hairy brown mane and it will look like a horse egg."

"What about me?" said Gideon.

"Here's one for you, Gideon. Give it a curved pair of horns and it will look like a goat egg," said Hetty.

So they all went away with their eggs.

In the morning, they met up again. Hetty was last to arrive. "Happy Eggday!" they said to one another, proudly showing off their eggs.

Hetty seemed the proudest of all as she showed them a beautiful, smooth, speckled egg. "I laid this especially!" she clucked. "Where's Dora?"

"Let's go and find Dora," said Humphrey.

They went along to the hayloft where Dora had made her nest.

"Dora! Dora!" called Pogson. "It's Eggday today! Come and

see my pig egg. My pig egg has a short curly tail."

"And my hen egg is smooth with brown speckles!" called Hetty.

"And my horse egg has a hairy brown mane!" called Humphrey.

"And my goat egg has a curved pair of horns!" called Gideon.

There was silence for a
while, then Dora started to quack. . .
"I've changed my mind," said Dora.
"It isn't Eggday anymore."
"Well, what day is it?"
asked Pogson.

"IT'S DUCKLING DAY!"

Dora quacked proudly.
And she lifted up her wing so that the
animals could peep underneath.

Well – you can guess who
had the best duckling!